JN076900

TOUCHING
MURASAKI SHIKIBU'S
SHOULDER

紫式部の肩に触れ

Poems in English and Japanese
Yasumori Sonoko

安森ソノ子 英日詩集

Translated by Kitagaki Muneharu
訳 北垣宗治

Coal Sack Publishing Company
Tokyo, Japan
コールサック社

TOUCHING MURASAKI SHIKIBU'S SHOULDER

紫式部の肩に触れ

Poems in English and Japanese

Yasumori Sonoko

安森ソノ子 英日詩集

Translated by Kitagaki Muneharu

訳　北垣宗治

Coal Sack Publishing Company
Tokyo, Japan
コールサック社

CONTENTS

III

The Translator's Introduction

TOUCHING MURASAKI SHIKIBU'S SHOULDER is a collection of Yasumori Sonoko's recent poems. I follow the Japanese custom of placing surname first and given name last. So Yasumori is her husband's surname and Sonoko her given name. Yasumori is a member of Japan P.E.N.Club, as well as of the Association of Japanese Poets. In this capacity she attended many international meetings, as her poems testify. She studied law at Doshisha University in Kyoto, and she used to teach social studies at high schools and colleges. She was one time a college librarian.

At the 23rd World Congress of Poets held in Osaka, she was honored by Poetry Prize for Excellency and a Certificate of Gratitude for Contribution in 2014. She has published poems and essays in Japan. She reads her own poems and other literary works on the stage, as well as radio and TV broadcasts.

The original of these poems are in Japanese. They were translated by Kitagaki Muneharu by her request. Kitagaki is an honorary professor of English at Doshisha University.

Characteristically Yasumori is a bold and courageous world traveler. This volume shows her experience in Paris, Oxford, Washigton, D.C., and New York City. She even traveled the Silk Road, visiting Kaxugar and the Taklamakan.

Yasumori was born in Kyoto, and currently lives close to the river Kamo, which is the Thames of London. Kyoto was Japan's ancient capital, 794-1868, and she was educated there and she loves Kyoto. Many of her poems are about Kyoto, and its environs, including Hanase and Kitayama. The River Kamo appears from time to time, in her poems. As a child she used to swim there. Thus, the River Kamo is the meeting-place for the departed spirits. Many citizens, who are nominally Buddhists take it for granted that on August 16, the following day of the Bon festival, all the departed spirits who had annual Bon reunion, must return to their former places, and the Five Hills of Kyoto customarily light bonfires at or after eight o'clock in the evening.

Yasumori's historical sense is remarkable in her poems. She loves Japanese classics such as *The Tale of Genji* by Murasaki Shkibu, whose tombstone is situated near her house. In the northern suburb of Kitayama (North Hiills), she recollects Taira no Kiyomori (1147-85), the hero of *The Tale of the Heike._*famous warrior of the latter part of the Heian period. In her Swiss poem she visits the Chateau de Chillon and she recites Byron's famous poem. Yasumori, an accomplished traditional Japanese dancer, presented her performance at an international meeting held at Kaxgar in the Silk Road!

Yasumori is fond of talking with foreign students. She seems to enjoy her conversation as her Oxford and Paris poems show. As poet's privilege she can listen to voices which fill the atmosphere. She has an excellent ear.

Yasumori loves history, especially the history of Kyoto. Kyoto is filled with historical memoris.

I am glad to say that translation of these poems helped the translator's understanding of not only the poems but the poet.

Muneharu Kitagaki
Honarary Professor, Doshisha University

September 5, 2019

I

Murasaki Shikibu Sitting

Blossoming bush clovers are all around me.
The wind blows lake-ward.
I hear the underground voice coming
From the shining surface of the lake to Ishiyama Temple.
It brings an ancient sound from the bottom of the ground.
I visit the temple—the sacred place where Lady Murasaki tackled
    her work.
I see a little doorway facing the east, leadng to her workshop.

The white wall keeps silence.
There Lady Murasaki sat, working.
She began to write *Tale of Genji*.
How she moved her intellectual eyes
On autumn nights she would have listened to the insects chorus,
And then gone out
She might have hesitated to begin the novel or not
With the rising moon she imagined men's evil passions
And their deepest thoughts, and she would have thought again,
Improving her work.

Here in Ishiyama Temple her portrait stands

This ancient building of Heian Period holds the most im-
    portant treasures
Lady Murasaki sitting is one.

1000 years ago
Writing and planning the long novel
She did feel the evening of her own life with sadness
She did feel sad and painful on a rainy night.
She was aware of her own death approaching.

I shut myself in my room, playing the koto.

Touching Murasaki Shikibu's Shoulder

Feeling the sign of autumn
I visit a nearby graveyard on Horikawa Street.
At the entrance to the yard
I am welcomed by "Lady Murasaki," a plant with full of small nuts
Of purple color; a butterfly flying on its leaves.
I proceed to the cool tombstone of Lady Murasaki.

With her head northward, Lady Murasaki is sleeping under the
    rectangular mound
Soft weeds and mosses cover the mound
I touch the mosses softly, as if touching Murasaki Shikibu's shoulder
Lady Murasaki's shoulder.

I say my gratitude in my prayer to the grave.
"I wrote poems, thinking of you.
I read *Tale of Genji* every day.
I read my papers in international meetings
And returned home safely.
Maybe you were guarding me, didn't you?"

Lady Murasaki appears in kimono of early autumn

Sitting in front of me, she gazes at me in clear look
"You are writing also; as a Heian writer I should like to talk
With you, a poet of the 21st century.
What shall we write and how shall we write.
There are many common topics between us."

Even if more than 1000 years passed
Under the same sky of Kyoto
Our conversasion still continues.

The Spirits in Kyoto

The Kamo River runs through Kyoto, my native town.
I swam in it in my childhood.
The river welcomed the water fowls
From Siberia in winter.
These white birds are my friends.

The birds come with spirits,
Who arrive on the wind blowing down from Mt. Hiei.
They are spirits of deceased members of my family.
They are sending their prayers to Kyoto,
They fill my heart with the words
Of my hope for the future.

Will the water fowls, the spirits, and I
Meet again some day
At the Kamo River in Kyoto?

Destiny

From the waves of Suma Beach the sound of flute is heard.
"What is that?"
It's Atsumori, the young prince of Heike clan
Playing his celebrated flute of Aoba,
The melody reaches the beach of the 21st century
The wind carries it to us gracefully.

The manly voice sounds from the sea:
"I was killed in the Battle of Ichinotani,
During the war between tha Genji clan and the Heike clan.
The Heike, my clan, was once in power
And helped to establish the new age of Samurai.
Our predecessor, the aristocrats were so corrupt
And the new order was surely due.
But we Heike was totally defeated by the Genji clan,
And the old Lady Tokuko, the grandmother of Emperor Antoku,
Holding the infant emperor, jumped into the sea, praying
'May there be a Miyako even at the sea-bottom.'"

Is it impossible to govern a country without war?
Is it destined a man in power must be driven out by the next man?

Patriotic passions must have been burning within him.

Whenever I hold my flute in my hands
I cannot help thinking of lives which were lost to no purpose.

Kyoto in the Last Days of the Tokugawa Shognate

On an early June morning
I awoke and found myself in a totally different world

I was a citizen of Kyoto but the year was 1864!
I was walking along the Takase River, in the evening
I saw samurais come and go busily,
An old single woman with grandchild, I was.
Suddenly, near Ikedaya Inn I heard shriekings in agony.
Four samurai of Shinsengumi Group,
Who were appointed to police the city by the Tokugawa
    Government
Raided the Ikedaya Inn to kill loyalists.
They were Kondo Isami, the captain of the group, and Okita Soji,
Nagakura Shinpachi, and Todo Heisuke.
Kondo called Sobei, the innkeeper and declared,
"We will inspect your inn."
Sobei got away from him upstairs, Kondo following him.
Kondo found about 20 loyalists were there.
The loyalsts drew their swords and ready to fight Kondo shouted,
    "No use struggling!"
Against him a loyalist raised his sword but Okita immediately

attacked and killed him.
Kondo and his company killed the loyalists one by one.
The Ikedaya Inn was
A battlefield abounding in bloodshed.
A loyalist who fell from the second-floor railing was stabbed
instantly
Todo was cut down by a samurai of Choshu, with blood in his eye.
Kondo met near death three times.
Finally Shinsengumi was victorious with the result of 14 dead;
arrested and executed 24 and escaped 11,
No more the loyalists could hold their secret meetings in the city.
They were awarded with 600 ryo by the Tokugawa Government.
Afterwards the government's search of the loyalists added severity.
Fierce battles continued in Kyoto: in order to drive out the Choshu
loyalists
They set fire on a citizen's house and the raging flames destroyed
811 wards, including 27513 houses
18 court nobles' houses, 51samurai houses, 253 Shiinto shrines and
Buddhist temples.
Two third of the city was lost.

The national seclusion policy was still alive
Even after Commodore Perry's black ships forced the door open.
Young patriots, realizing national crisis, were quite active.
One of them, Sakamoto Ryoma, was conspicuous in concluding a
    military alliance
Between Choshu domain and Satsuma domain, the two leading
    domains
But Sakamoto was killed in Kyoto at the age of 33.
Led by the two domains they were successful in establishing the
    new imperial government

Born and raised in Kyoto, I imagine the heads
Gibbeted and exposed, but I look up to the gentle Higashiyama
    Hills to the east.

Tokugawa Shogunate ended and Tokyo became the new capital
Water birds stand in line on the bank of the Kamo River .
They are the spirits of the departed souls.
Their farewell songs, written on strips of paper
May have sunk in the shallow Takase River.
Their voices are unheard,
They reach only mind's ear of sensitive people.

Circumstances of Kyoto- the Kamo River

Disturbed by the river sound
But I enjoy the sound.
In this space of my study
I appreciate the energy of the water and
The time, which is flowing into eternity.

Across the width of the river
The water falls in white.
This is the grand screen which welcomes the water birds.
On the shallows of frothy waves
I sink both devil's female mask and angel mask
In late autumn I sit on the river bank alone
I recollect the deceased members of my family.
Overwhelmed by the stream's power.

In the sunshine
The expression the running water,
The view of my birthplace, the blue soul,
The prayer of the dead
Who continue to show a scroll of writing
In the sky;

The Kyoto of my dead ancestors
May live on.

Great circumstances of Kyoto
Holds the dreams for the future.
This city—my birthplace
I pray for its immortality.

The House Which I Must Protect

Although I am not living there
I must protect it; a heavy pressure for me.
Despite my intension not to live there
I find peace of mind wafting through the air.

The house and its garden were designed carefully by my grandfather
Who was born towards the end of Edo period.
The pattern of rice-fields was worked into its layout intelligently.
Winds pass through from the front garden to the back garden.
The north/south winds cross the east/west breeds in the living room.
One can enjoy the cool and birdsongs.

The house looks like the house where Basho, the haiku poet was born.
I wish I have my own study in front of the storehouse in the back
    garden
As my summer house. I cannot forget the big golden carps in the
    pond.

The old persimmon tree, together with grasshoppers at my feet,
    whisper:
"It's out of date for you to live in the house

Though your ancestor lived here as a guardian,
Crossing the mountain pass 830 meters high
No more inhabited, but you can keep your presence of mind with smile
The old house will somehow endure and survive snow
Only be careful of leaky ceiling.
You are the caretaker."

I am enjoying every convenience of a city life.
I have lived by the sweat of my brow both in the country and the city
Advanced age hears an advice.
Difficult way, but I am pushed from behind towards a possible step.

An Ancient Plant in a Kyoto Pond

The pond is called Midorogaike,
Where grows buck bean, a medical herb 30 million years old.
The pond with a circumference of 1.5 kilo meters
Has an island which appears to be afloat.
Spring comes to the floating island and the spirit of the water singing
    to the sky.

The white blossoms of the buck bean are in white flame
Shining all together.

The fossilized seeds of buck bean were discovered in West Siberia
    recently
The low hills surrounding the quiet pond
Have protected the buck bean

Who dumped a black bass into this pond?
This foreign fish is distributed throughout the northern hemisphere
The buck bean works well for stomach troubles

Japan is an island country in the Far East,
And the pond is situated in the north of Kyoto.

The temperature of the water does not change
So, even though a peculiar fish like black bass strays in
The pond is all right, with the buck bean blossoms in May.
The peat under the floating island helps aboriginal.

Hanase Pass

I heard the breathing of the mountains at the Pass.
The opposite slope of the valley was studded by
The white flowers of magnolia kobus.
The coppice was singing intently of the fresh green.

I came to know the secret of water there.
It flicks on the surface under cedar wood, and slips into the earth
Goes down, moistening the mountainside from within,
And appears again, gushing in torrent from fault.
The water springing clear and cool without end.
It keeps its excellent taste, perhaps a result of the pressure of the
    heavy snow
Every one covets the blue cold water who knows its taste.

I heard the change of the wind at the Pass.
The word wavers delicately from day to day
Why did they install AMeDAS ?
Driving my car against critically stormy night
I came to realize the reason, passing Hanase Pass.

I thought of the hope of a large city at the Pass.

I saw air pollution over the far-away city of day-times
The mountains and water since the ancient times
Sympathized each other secretly.
The Pass understands this
Detached, keeping his own independence.

The Mountain Road of Kita-Yama

When I read aloud *The Tale of Heike*, I become the book's
   contemporary.
Taira-no-Kiyomori walked deep into the inner part of Northern
   Kyoto via mountain road of my native village
I am walking now the same mountain road as Kiyomori passed.
Now it is a narrow road, but Kiyomori did pass it in the twelfth
   century.

There is an old building Kiyomori constructed deep in the
   Kita-Yama.
It is said to be the prototype of the famous veranda of Kiyomizu
   Temple.
It tells me of the strong hope the ancient tradition of the mountain
   worship of Japan.
Kiyomori and I are discussing the kokoro (mind/heart) of Japanese.

II

Global Warming

These unusual occurrences in the ecosystem
The sun watches closely.
The magma in the bowels of the earth is storing anger day by day
The wind sighs.

Is human intellect heading in such a cruel direction?
Animals and plants deplore and are bewildered
The mysterious aura of the earth becomes weaker year by year
Pressed by the audacity of nuclear weapons

"Our country will sink into the sea,
In the future this earth might vanish."
I hear this sorrowful voice from the ocean.
The voice wanders in the sky.
Even in the process of the progress of civilization and the simple daily
    life
Aim at coexistence as their summit
There is a hellish ant pit.
Under an aspiration a faint hope and light flickering.

Nomonhan Incident

The horizon is far away on the Steppes
Gigantic clouds spread overhead from Gobi Desert.
A terrible military collision took place between Soviet and Japanese
   armies
In 1939, just two years before the outbreak of the Pacific War.
It's called Nomonhan Incident.
Nomonhan was a border town between Manchuria and Mongol
   People's Republic.
Manchuria was a puppet country, the Imperialist Japan fabricated.

I was not born yet, when the question was at issue.
The cease-fire agreement was reached in September, 1939.
Can I enjoy this splendid view without recalling its date?
My country did invade the Continent.
Under the refreshing sky in the peaceful present situation
We are enjoying Mongol tour, but
The soldiers who fell here must have left the repeated voices of
   homesickness.

The Flower at the Silk Road

I have been familiar with zinnia since my childhood.
I met the rouge-colored zinnia unexpectedly on the foot of Tian Shan
    Mountains
As if it were waiting for me to come.
It's called in Japanese hyakunichiso (plant for a hundred days) because
It keeps desire for a hundred days without crumbling.
With its strong stalk straight of the annual plant.

When a child I had a small box of expectation for the next year,
A box for the seeds.
The box kept black zinnia seeds even smaller than sesame
They opened pink, scarlet, or whitish flowers with crystal dew.
The y were heroines in a Kyoto village 600 meters above the sea-level.
They were hostesses in the banquet of my garden.

One summer I joined an open air meeting of poetry recitation.
With the farawy Tenchi Lake with the surface of the lake 1980 meters
    above the sea level.,
I came to Urmchi, travelling through the Silk Road.
The zinnia of the place knew human passion boiling within.
They had inner shrines.

The breathing
Led me toward overcoming pain.
Breathing led me towards overcoming of pain.

Reading at Kaxgar

Kaxgar is an oasis city 1200 meters high above the sea-level.

In my favorite kimono and my dancing fan in my hand
My familiar music, together witlh my poems begin to walk on the
 stage
The sound of my heart I recorded in Kyoto I hear on the Continent
 of Asia.

Mr. O, my Chinese guide studied Japanese literature in a Japanese
 college.
He read aloud a classic for us in his deep voice
It was quite impressive to listen to a Japanese masterpiece abroad.
"The Japanese classic is thriving here," I felt.

At the westernmost city of the Chinese Republic,
Facing the wind blowing from the Silk Road
I thought of the ups and downs of realized exchange between Japan
 and China
In this city of busy traffic, where live so many Uigurs
Footsteps sound of historic cities of culture and castles
And urge to have eyes to look into literary abyss.

Dance at Shangrila

The breeze from the Tibetan Cultural Sphere brought an invitation
A proposal that each participating country should present native
    dance.
Thus I was obliged to present a Japanese dance.

I left Japan for Yungang well-prepared for stage.
I had a black crested kimono and a yellow *hakama** in my suitcase.

Dance was a part of formal program of the Asia Poet Congress,
The eyes of all the participants were focused on the Japanese dancer.
The dancer from Kyoto did feel their expectation.
She moved on the colorful stage slowly.
In this foreign country
It was fitting for samurai to express the spirit deeply and inspiringly
According as an unbroken tradition.

The dance ended. Suddenly a voice shouted, "I want the photo of
    your dance!"
The voice came from the back row. It was a young native boy.
He hurried out of the hall.
Now I do have the photo to send him still, but his address is
    unknown.

Young man, your interest in Japan may come into bloom in the
    future.
I too, am dreaming the day.

I see clouds are moving toward the Continent.
I send my message to the boy through the clouds.

    Hakama is a long pleated skirt worn over a kimono.

The Dance on the Stage

The tip of the folding fan points the way.
In the distance humans walk a steady pace,
Our hopes spread before us.

The pleasures of life, suffering,
    jarring reality are fused together,
And I become a dancing body.

I return the fan to my breast after folding it closed.
The fire of life lit by the dance warms my body,
Brings forth a fresh stream of blood,
    and marks the passage of time.

The fan knows everything;
    it pushes me forward and judges my heart.
The fan instructs me to raise a light
    at the peak of the mountain of art.

The Boy at the Taklamakan Desert

The temperature of the surface of the earth sinks deep into my sole,
The extension of the hot sand in the Taklamakan
I am melting into

I wish to go to the small hill top
The driving boy returns to me from the hill, saying,
" Please everybody, go aboard.
I'll conduct you to that hill,"
He lets us stand on the old wooden rack on his donkey.
He inspects us the sight-seers who come from every corner of the
    world.
He looks astonishly young as graduated from a primary school
    yesterday.
He gazes at his donkey who was working without rest.

The boy gives his donkey the first whip into moving.
The donkey's steps slowly with rackful guests on,
The boy gives continuous whips to the donkey,
Which gives the animal a faithful breath, which sounds like
Phantom clear stream in Tian Shan mountains,
A rooter's song, saying

"There should be some day when a cool wind may blow from Tian
    Shan."
In Tarim Basin, in this Interior of the Northern Hemisphere
The donkey and men are united in the journey.

The single-minded pace of the donkey on the scorching sand
Makes my hands move rhythmically with gratitude.

III

Toward Oxford

After Paris and London I'm on my way to Oxford...
I am rocked from side to side in a train bound for Oxford alone
I find a small table facing the opposite seat
I can open my notebook on it
And I can also write letters without difficulty.
The outside green of the suburbs sends fragrance of the country to us.
A poem flashes suddenly.

I hear Byron's voice when I straighten up myself in my seat.
The voice sounds sonorously: "Eternal Spirit of the chainless Mind!
Brightest in dungeons, Liberty! Thou art;—
For there thy habitation is the heart—
The heart which love of thee alone can bind.

Lord Byron visited the Chillon Castle in Switzerland in 1816.
He sang of Bonnyvard, the Genevan reformist
The spirit who cried for political liberty and religious reform.
Byron dedicated his surging passion to his memory.

A strong humanitarian thought invites me toward the academic town
Full of students. Deeply I think of liberty in the train.

The moving train for me is my study where I can think—
The limited time, yet so precious.

On the Oxford Campus

In a quiet afternoon on campus
I met a tall studeint, and talked. Blinking his blue eyes he said:
"To study together with students from various countries
Is a precious moment for me.
I would like to discuss the problem of each country as it is.
We do have interest in Asia, but I have never been to Japan.
I do wish to visit Asian countries including Japan."

"Both Japan and England are surrounded by the seas geographically.
To say nothing of our tortuous history, we share the destiny of island
    nation.
The urgent question we face is how to survive the present situation.
I would like to discuss such problems with students from abroad.
Am I dreaming?"

"We no longer depend on ships or rail. This is the age of aeroplane.
We should think of the safety of flight.
To obey the international laws is perhaps more important.
Despite the difference of religion and national philosophy,
We should try to understand each other, hoping a better tomorrow."

Thus ran the conversation between the young student and a Kyoto
  poet,
A visitor from Kyoto who is also a mother of two children.
They are good friends under the May sky of Oxford.

The Boy at his Mother's Breast

He came
Dart-like upon us.
A group of tourists young and old
Visiting Lake Como.

Pretending to pass the oldest Japanese gentleman
He hit him and left; but he failed.
The wallet in his trousers pocket was all right.
The only spoils were an old watch and chain and a key.

The mother sat by the roadside suckling her baby.
The little boy, aged maybe seven or eight, with white skin and
    brown hair,
In his charming jeans, looked pure and innocent,
His daily task was to pickpocket some cash in this way.

We all have a sad sky.
O, Boy, show your mother the purity of your heart.
Protect your brother and sister.
Foster the just and upright spirit and look up the sky.
Accept your destiny with dignified attitude.
Leave your fine legacy in friendship on earth,

Do live on and on!

Let us look straight into eyes each other,
Let us go beyond the mountains together.

Toward Evening at Quartier Latin

A voice of phantom says to haul in the star—
It is toward evening at Quartier Latin.
The french language, English and Kyoto dialect are mixed and
   combined in my mind.
Quite relieved, I sit on a chair nearby in this students town.
I remember a French youth, whom I met for an interview a long
   time ago
He was studying political science
"I do want," he said, "to visit China and Japan in the future."
What is he doing now? I wonder.

The interview took place on campus of the Paris University in the
   month of May.
A beautiful girl friend was sitting next him.
They may have married and they may be struggling in life.
Perhaps he is a professor by now.

No matter what status he got in his society, I do want
To meet him and hear from him what he really thinks about Japan
   and the Japanese.
Alas, I have no means to contact him.

I do not know his full name or his university.

The son of my sister's daughter went to study to the University of Paris
    last year.
If he happens to remember the fact that I too studied political science
    in Japan,
If he remembers this from his ocean of memory!

Impossible? Hopeless?
Human encounter, like stars in constellations, however brilliant and
    mysterious,
Just flows away.

A Visit to the United Nations

The land mine in front of me
Is round and of orange color.
I watch the weapon in exhibition intently which can give
Bodily and fatal wounds to one who steps on it.
I now realize the real shape of the mine.

The weapon blows up anybody who steps on it.
Rather than killing men, its effect is more grievous
Than death; the wounded sufferers' pain lasts for ages.
A number of mins are still under ground long after the war.

The earth turns round still
These terrible weapons under ground although
Campaign for removal of them are on the way by volunteers.
What are the words of the sleepers in the ground?

"The ill-omened unfolding" as Estimate.
Mines are set where the enemy army are expected to pass.
They react the weight of steps,
They also react to quakes.
Their triggering devices are so delicate.

Visiting the United Nations in New York
I felt my own body is filled by mines.
The fact is that about 110 million mines are still asleep in the earth,
The information made me tremble in the afternoon on Manhattan.

A Visit to Washington, D. C.

I visited Washington, D. C. from New York by air.
The Japanese guide who was waiting for us at the airport began
His job in his automobile after giving us a general explanation.

He guided us the three Japanese the whole day.
While walking he explained on what fundamental principle the
    country was built.
This city is an artificial town along with a plan.
I looked around at the scenes in pastel and found a river somewhat
    resembling the River Kamo.
What did I see, and what did I think?

The White House was built in 1800.
It was shining whitely, made of Virginia gray limestone.
George Washington, the first president, did the foundation work in
    1792

In the Lincoln Memorial I found that dear memorable passage
"That government of the people, by the people, for the people"
Which recollected the days of English beginners as I was one.

At the Arlington National Cemetery I offered my condolences to

The patriots who died for the country.
Their voice expanding within me with increasing loudness
Telling their spiritual paths to their destiny.

I finally was successful in visiting the National Air and Space Museum
Of the Smithsonian Institution. I saw the rock which was brought
     from the moon.
I had a conversation with it—an unforgettable fact and unspeakable
     thought.

The moon rock was brought back by the space pilot.
Why did I stand still with my eyes fastened to it?
Thanks to the wisdom of humankind
The rock on the surface of the moon
Contrary to our imagination, however beautiful,
However heavy, taken off by human agency.
It moved from the moon, and found a new residence in my heart.

At the University of Paris

Leaving Switzerland I came to Paris,
I had an appointment for an interview at the University of Paris.
A political science student came to see me and spoke his dream of the
    future
My notes of the interview are still kept in my desk.
That was May of the year 1987.

Another young man entered this same university in 2015
Whose father a French and mother a Japanese.
He thinks of his mother's birthplace, Kyoto.

"Perhaps" says he, "blood connects me to Kyoto.
The younger sister of my mother's mother wrote a book.
It was on sale in a nearby bookstore in Paris
Its green cover impressed me.
Half of my blood is Japanese. Japan, my Maman's country, is not far.
Let us talk about the times we share together."

Afterword

In April 2016, I published a collection of poems by "Dancing in Shangri-La". Since then, I have wanted to leave a considerable number of works of poetry written in Asian countries, Europe and America in English.

Along with recent poetry work, several work from "Dancing in Shangri-La" were placed on the desk, and the poems written in Japanese were described in English. One day followed a day that imposed me to finish writing one work a day in English for myself.

Since attending the 47th International P.E.N. Congress Tokyo 36 years ago, I had been in a state of having a world literary congress with literary figures from around the world, and have become willing to publish in both English and Japanese. My experience in which I have recited and given speeches at East Asian poetry meetings, Asian Poets Conferences, and World Congress of Poets is still utilized at the World Congress of Poets that is held every two years, and each time I repeat the opportunity to participate, it deepens as my diverse expression fields such as reading my own poems, lectures on research themes, performing traditional Japanese dances, etc.

The world situation changes, and various voices from far away from the earth still make us think about the country, society and people.

I am going to send this collection of poems with great gratitude to my old friends, poetry friends who have always worked together, and people around the world who are talking together at the World Congress of Poets.

On this planet of the solar system, I will ponder the meaning of the relationship of living together in the present era, and I hope to describe the culture and civilization further facing in the heart of this earth and want to describe it remembering my beginner's mind.

I owed Prof. Muneharu Kitagaki of my alma mater a lot as I was a law graduate who wanted to publish English poetry. It is a distinct honor that he finally translated my poems from Japanese into English..

I would also like to express my sincere gratitude to Mr. Hisao Suzuki, President of Coal Sack and all the people who have taken care of me.

November 24, 2019
Sonoko Yasumori

Author Career

Sonoko Yasumori (maiden name: Sonoko Fujii)

Born in Kyoto City

1963 Graduated from Doshisha University, Faculty of Law, Department of Political Science. Trained at Kyoto University from the same year. From 1960 to 2000, she presented her research at the "Ie no Kai" in Kyoto (including literary theory). The half of the period was the caretaker representative until 2000.

1979 Poetry collection "Shiso o Tsumu (Picking Perilla) " (Book Publisher : Poetry Center)Became a Japan Library Association selected book

1982 "Japanese Contemporary Women's Poetry Collection: Sonoko Yasumori Poetry Collection" (Book Publisher : Geifu Shoin)

1989 "Women Choral Suite by Sonoko Yasumori's Poetry, Shiso o Tsumu Toki (When Picking Perilla)" (Book Publisher : ONGAKUNO TOMO SHA Corp.)

1996 Poetry collection "Chijo no Jikoku (Time on Earth)" (Book Publisher : Henshu-kobo Noah)

1997 Collection of essays "Kyoto Rekishi no Tsumugiito (Kyoto History Spinning yarn)" (Book Publisher : Kantosha)

2008 "Soprano song collection with poetry by Sonoko Yasumori, Kyoto o Togu (sharpening Kyoto)" (Book Publisher : Maizono project)

2016 Poetry collection "Dancing in Shangri-La" (Book Publisher : Doyou Bijutsu-sha Shuppan Hanbai)

2018 E-book "Dancing in Shangri-La" (Book Publisher : Oikaze Shobo)
CD release of "Women Chorus by Sonoko Yasumori's Poetry", "Soprano Song by Sonoko Yasumori's poetry, Kyoto o Togu (Sharpening Kyoto)".

Affiliation

Japan Pen Club (received a membership award of long service for 35 years, former committee member), Member of Japan Poets Association, The Japan Poets Club, Kansai Poets' Association, Gendai Kyoto Shiwakai (Contemporary Kyoto

Poetry Association), Kyoto Arts and Culture Foundation, Kyoto Japan-France Association, NPO Kyoto Community Broadcasting, and Pandora Collection of Poems in English and Japanese.

Career and activities history
Reporting, Writing and Former councilor at the Scientific Society of Thoughts. Former teacher at high school and university. Former library director at university. Writing at the University of Paris and Oxford University.
Modern Japan Gold Academy representative.
Planned and broadcasting now "Sonoko Yasumori's Poetry and Essay" at FM79.7 Kyoto Sanjo Radio Cafe of Kyoto Community Broadcasting.

Poetry magazines
"Breath" "PANDORA" (published in Japanese and English) coterie.
Former "Earth" "Fence" the cessation of publication. Former Japan futurism coterie.

Awards
2014 "Poetry Prize for Excellency" and "Certificate of Gratitude for a Contribution" at the World Congress of Poets.
2018 "Modern Japan Literature Writers Award"
2019 "France Arts and Culture Award"

Qualification of dance teacher
Became a certified lecturer of the All Japanese Folk Dance Association (Stage name: Fugetsu Maisono).
Learned Seiga-ryu school of Kenbu (sword dance) (Pseudonym: Fumika Yasumori), and classical dance by Hanayagi-ryu school.
She has been on stage in Noh Theater since her 20s at Noh Kanze-ryu school, and she studied under Teiji Kawamura (an important intangible cultural property holder as a member of the Kanze-ryu school). Currently, she studies under Kazushige Kawamura (Kanze-ryu school Shitekata (main roles), head of Kawamura Noh Stage). At the World Congress of Poets, she was in charge of her own poetry presentation, small lecture, and Japanese dance presentation.She attends and makes presentations almost every time at the Asian Poets Conference.
Home: 29 Shimoitakura-cho, Koyama, Kita-ku,Kyoto-shi, 603-8124, JAPAN

目次

三章

翻訳者序

　詩集『紫式部の肩に触れ』は安森ソノ子さんの最近の詩を集めたもので
ある。私は日本のしきたりに従い姓を先に、名を後に書く。それで安森は
彼女の夫の姓であり、ソノ子が親からつけられた名前である。安森さんは
日本ペン・クラブの会員であり、日本詩人クラブ等の会員でもある。その
資格で彼女は多くの国際会議に出席した事は内容の示す通りである。彼女
は京都の同志社大学法学部の出身で、高校や大学で教えて来た。彼女はさ
る大学の図書館長を務めたこともある。

　彼女は 2014 年に大阪で開催された第 23 回世界詩人会議で、優秀な詩と
ともにその貢献に感謝する栄誉賞が贈られた。彼女は詩集を発行するかた
わら、詩の朗読を行い、ラジオやテレビで放送・放映されてきた。

　原詩はすべて日本語で書かれている。彼女の願いにより北垣宗治が翻訳
した。北垣は同志社大学名誉教授である。

　安森さんは大胆で、勇気のある世界旅行者であることを特色とする。こ
の詩集は彼女がパリ、オックスフォード、ワシントン D. C.、ニューヨーク
市で経験したことを述べている。彼女の旅行範囲はシルクロードのカシュ
ガルからタクラマカン砂漠にまで及んでいる。

　安森さんは京都生まれである。今も鴨川の近くに住んでいる。鴨川はロ
ンドンのテームズ川に当る。京都は日本の古都（794-1868）だった。彼女
は京都で教育を受けたし、彼女は京都を愛している。多くの詩は京都なら
びに京都近郊に関するものである。例えば花背や北山のごとく。鴨川は彼
女の詩に時々出てくる。子供の頃鴨川で泳いだという。鴨川は彼女にとり
死者の霊の相合う場所なのである。お盆のあくる日（8 月 16 日）には、お
盆に帰ってきた死者の霊たちが元の場所に帰る日であり、京都では五山で

送り火の行事が午後8時以後に行われる。これは京都の風物詩であり、仏教徒でない人びともこの行事を楽しむ。

　これらの詩には安森さんの歴史感覚が顕著に表れている。彼女は紫式部の『源氏物語』が好きである。式部の墓が彼女の家の近くにある。北山で彼女は『平家物語』の英雄である平清盛（1147–85）を思い出す。彼女はスイスでシヨンの城を訪ねたことがある。そしてバイロンの有名な詩を朗誦する。安森さんは日本舞踊の名手でもある。シルクロードのカシュガルで国際会議が開かれた時、会場で日本舞踊を披露して、喝さいを博した。

　安森さんは外国の学生と話すことが好きである。詩人の特権として空中に漂っている声を聞くことができる。彼女は優れた耳を持つ。

　これらの詩を英訳してみて、詩を理解しただけでなく、詩人をも理解できたことは、望外の喜びだった。

北垣宗治
同志社大学名誉教授

2019 年 9 月 5 日

紫式部が座っている

いちめんの　咲き揺れる萩の花
風は湖へ
みずうみから石山寺へと　地底の声を運んでいる
湖国の十一面観音展を見た晴れた日に
訪れた　紫式部が筆を持った地
東へ向かい夢誘う小さな出入り口
朽ちかけた木に　白壁の沈黙ほのぼのと
奥に座した紫式部は
源氏物語の筆をおこすまで
どんなに知的な瞳をうつろわせていたことだろう
秋の宵　聞こえる虫の音に表へ出
筆を折ろうと悩みぬき
登る月の光に　醜い煩悩を洗い流せない人びとをはかなんだことだろう

御堂の中に紫式部画像
藤原時代の建築　映える寺宝の数かず
抹香の煙　金色と化し
厨子内の如意輪観音を幾重にもとりまいている
どのような時代にも　変らなかった仏の下に
眠る人さまざまのにくしみ　愁い

それらを〝雨夜の品定め〟のように
今　宴席の隣の友であるように

洒脱に語る式部の想い
長編を綴る手もとに
人生の黄昏の悲しさが宿っていくことを
雨の夜の切なさを
平安時代に宴の宵を架空につくり　耐え
やがて　現世から失せる身であるゆえに書いたことを
知ってきびしく
　　　　　　　私の
──琴を弾く──

紫式部の肩に触れ

秋の気配を身に受けて
詣でたのは　紫式部の墓
住む地に近い堀川通りに面した入口で
紫の小さな実がぴっしりと寄りそい
葉にしじみ蝶舞うムラサキシキブに迎えられ
涼しげな奥へと進む

北の方を枕とし
長方形のこんもりとした盛り上がりの下に
先人は眠る
広いのびのびとした土の盛り上がりに　やわらかな雑草　短い杉苔
　　が生え
私は　紫式部の肩に触れる思いで
杉苔の上に　そっと手を置く

報告と感謝の念が　土中へとしみていく
「あなたを想い詩を書き　源氏物語を日々読み込み　異国で発表をし
　　てきました
無事　世界大会で担当を終え　帰国しました
見守って下さったのですね」と手をあわせる

紫式部は　初秋の着物姿で現れて
澄んだ眼差しで　私の前に座る

「あなたも筆をもつならば　平安時代に書いていた私は　平成三十年
　の現世人と話合いたい
何をどう書くか　共通の話題はいっぱいで」

千年余を経ても　同じ京都の空の下
胸に会話が積っていく

霊は京都で

生地のせせらぎ　鴨川は
幼い頃の水泳場
冬にはシベリアから戻る水鳥を迎え
白い飛鳥は私の仲間

比叡下しの風に乗り
水鳥の背後に霊が
故人となった家族が
今の京都に　望みを送る
表現を想う私に　未来の書状を託している
水鳥と霊と私
再会する場所は京都の鴨川

運命

須磨の浜辺の波間より
聞こえる　笛の音
〝あれは？〟

十六歳で戦死した敦盛の吹く音色
笛の名手であった若き公達の
天上から吹く青葉の笛が
二十一世紀の浜辺に届く
風の運ぶ旋律　みやびやかに

海上からの声　凛としてひびく
　源平の戦い　一の谷の合戦で私は討たれた
　貴族社会の腐敗を振り払い
　武士の支配する世を培った我等平家
　だが宿敵源氏の軍勢に破れ
　海の藻屑と消えた時
　「波の下にも　都はあろうぞ」と
　幼い安徳天皇は祖母に抱かれ
　海中へ消えた
　戦いを避けずして　世は治まらなかったのか
　いや権力を一旦握った者は　次の権力者に
　座を追われる運命にあるのか
　国を想う情熱は　それぞれの胸に燃えたぎっていて

私は笛を手にする度に
限りなく現世の人々の　尊い命を想っている
笛を愛する日常で
人の世の知恵ある活力と向き合っている
実在の肉体は消えようとも
心にしみる香ばしい音　芸術の魂を

幕末の京

六月の早朝
目覚めると　前日までの風景は一変し
一四〇年程前の　京の街が広がっている
夕ぐれ時に　高瀬川のほとりへ出かけた
幕末の志士達が行き交う京都の木屋町
池田屋という旅宿のそばを　女一人
子を育て　孫をもつ身の私は　歩いていた

高瀬川にかかる橋を渡ろうとした瞬間　恐ろしい騒動を見てしまっ
　たのだ
元治元年・一八六四年六月五日であった
幕府より京の街の取締りを命じられていた新選組の四人が　三条木
　屋町に近い池田屋へ　突如飛び込んで行った
新撰組の局長・近藤勇と隊士の沖田総司　永倉新八　藤堂平助の四
　人が池田屋を襲撃した

近藤勇は　池田屋の主人惣兵衛を呼び出して
「今宵、旅宿御改めであるぞ！」と言い
奥に二階へ逃げ込んだ主人のあとを追うと
そこには幕府に反対し　世の中をたて直そうと企む志士二十名ばか
　りがいた
急な事態　志士たちはいっせいに刀をぬき
何者が来たのかと身構えている

近藤勇は「御用御改め、手向いいたすにおいては、容赦なく斬り捨
　　てる」と叫ぶ
志士の一人が勇敢にも斬りかかると　新選組の沖田がすかさず斬り
　　倒し　池田屋で密会をしていた志士たちを次々と倒して行った
寺田屋は斬り合い　合戦の場となり　血しぶきが飛ぶ　流れる
2階から落ちてきた志士を　新選組隊士は　突き刺す
藤堂は　長州の志士に斬られ　目に血が入っている
近藤は三度も斬られそうになっている
そこへ　同じく新選組の土方隊が突入して　生き地獄の有様　新選
　　組は勝つ結果となったこの事件　関連の秘密集会も含め　死者
　　十四名　捕えられた後の処刑　病死二十四名　逃亡した者十一名
　　であった
幕府打倒の密会現場にいた尊攘急進派志士たちを斬り殺したとして
　　　褒賞金六百両が　幕府から　当日池田屋で戦った新選組の隊士
　　達に支払われた
平成の時代では　約一八〇〇万円に相当する池田屋での事件を経て
　　　幕府による不呈浪士の探索は　ますます厳しくなる
京都での激戦は続き　とうとう京都市街は火の海となる禁門の変を
　　迎えた
長州兵一掃のため放火された火は　三日間燃え続けた
消失被害は町数八百十一町　世帯数二万七千五百十三軒　公家屋敷
　　十八　武家屋敷五十一　社寺二百五十三　市中の三分の二を焼失
　　した

黒船が日本へ来て以来の鎖国体制の行きづまり

政局は混沌とし　国家の行方を真剣に心配する若人の群

坂本龍馬は三十三歳で京都で刺客に襲われ他界するまで　日本のために奔走する

慶応二年・一八六六年　薩摩と長州はついに軍事同盟を結ぶ

身分制度にしばられていた日本は　大政奉還　明治維新へと困難な政情を一新していく

生まれ育った京の街で　どれだけ殺戮の場を見てきたことか

殺された人間の生首が次々とさらされた京の鴨川の岸辺で　私はなだらかな東山を仰いだ

幕末の京の街　鴨川には水鳥が過去の人々の霊を抱くように　黙して　並ぶ

高瀬川の浅い川底には　死者の無念の辞世の句が　人知れず沈んでいる

その静けさに　耳をかたむけよう

同志社大学西門で

烏丸通りに面した門
通い慣れた母校の西門
ふるさとの風景の一地点に
「薩摩藩邸跡」　と立つ表示

十八歳で入学した頃
この遺跡表示は無かった
幕末史に目を凝らすようになり
身近に語りかける刻まれた文字
「薩摩藩　ようがんばらはった」
坂本龍馬を研究する中で
薩長連合への動きの足音　幕末の志士の胸中
炎と化して　令和元年の衣服に飛ぶ

坂本龍馬　西郷隆盛　多くの先達
あなた達の　"日本を洗い直す"という信念のもと
歴史は迎えた　明治維新を

西門の前で
わが身は　自然に動き出す
刀をもって城山で自死に至る西郷隆盛の姿になりきる
矢も尽き　ふるさとの城山で命を絶たねばならなかっ
　　た西郷の呼吸は

人間の最期を受け入れる決意を
〈毅然〉と後世に伝え

予想外の無念の死
暗殺された坂本龍馬の
常に日本全体を視野に置いた眼光
母校の西門で　今日の私を見すえる

新島襄の書

墨の濃淡
のびやかに語る文字の呼吸
筆の跳ねる力に

「一度志したならば　貫けよ　人としての誠意の道を」
　　と宙からの声　重なり
振り返る　七十八年の日々を

描く
残された寿命での私の坂道を

鴨川で

流れの音に遮断され
響きをＢＧＭに
作る空間　この書斎
水の活力は
残る時間と永却の淵を示し
語り続けて

川幅一杯の白い落下は
水鳥を迎える大スクリーン
泡散る浅瀬に
般若の面も小面も沈ませて
晩秋　一人岸辺の
難路の地図帳
流れの奏でる底力に
亡くした家族の
京都を研ぐ

陽光のもと
渡る水の面の表情
生地の川　青の霊
死者ののぞみは
空の書状の帯を
流し続けて

この環境よ
未来への夢抱き
ふるさとの京の街
永遠に

守るべき家

今は　住んでもいないのに
全身の重しになっている
住む気はなくとも
どこかにただよう　安らぎ　落ちつき

江戸時代末に生まれた祖父が
考え慎重に設計した田舎の屋敷　庭
田の字型　昔からの農村の合理的な間取り
風は表庭から裏庭へ通り　南北からの風と
東西の広緑からの微風は
居間の真中で交差する
涼しい居心地　野鳥の鳴声

松尾芭蕉の生家と似ている！
裏庭の土蔵の前に　自分だけの書斎をもてば良いのだ
池の金色の太った鯉の思い出と共に
夏に使う別宅として　今後も

明治時代から見守る柿の木と
足もとのキリギリスは　語る
「旧式な家を守って村に住み
八三〇メートル余の峠越えで
エネルギーをいつも費やすのは時代に合わない

過去の家は無人となったが、どっしりと笑顔で居よう
親の旧居は風雨　大雪になんとか耐えるよ
でも家の中へ水漏れをさせては　おしまい
大屋根の修理は必ずせよ
管理は　あなたの任務だ」

街の家の便利さは
都市と田舎で汗を流してきた身体をつつみ込み
高齢者のわが耳へ　助言を送る
困難な道　可能な歩みへ
背を押す

自生の薬草

氷河時代からの植物を自生させて迎える
水面
周囲一・五メートルの深泥池
真中に浮く浮島に　春がきて
水の精霊　空に歌う
三千万年前からの薬草のミツガシワが
白い花の炎となって
いっせいに光る想いと共に

西シベリアで発見された
三千万年前の種子　ミツガシワの化石
静まる池を抱く小高い山は
ミツガシワを守り　仰ぐ
種子の先輩と語る

ブラックバス
誰が放したのか　外国のこの魚を
極地周辺の北半球に分布する
古来からの胃のもたれ　腹痛に効く
薬草ミツガシワの　春毎に生える池へ

極東の島日本の　京都の北部
国指定天然記念物

深泥池の変わらない水温は
突拍子もない魚が泳いできても
浮島の中　泥炭のもとで
五月毎に花を優雅に咲かせるであろう
温帯地帯の　この不思議な現象
池は不変

花背峠

山の呼吸を　峠で聴いた
谷をへだてた向いの斜面
辛夷の花は点在し
雑木林は　胸いっぱいの新緑を歌う

川の雫を　峠で知った
水はちろちろと杉林の地に　表れ
傾斜をひたして　峠を下り
再び地下へもぐった
そして峠下　山の断層からとうとうと流れ出した
冷たく澄んだ湧き水　絶えることなく美味しく
冬の大雪に耐える山地
アイスブルーの水は　知る人のみ知る超人気

風の変化を峠で聞いた
風が運ぶ四季の明暗
日毎の言葉は微妙に揺れ
「アメダス」が置かれた謂れを
風雨の宵に　吹き飛ばされそうになって識った
雷雨の中を　ハンドルを握った峠越えで知った

都会の望みを　峠で諳った
大気の汚染を　かなたの昼の街に見た

古代からの山と水
生きる命の生涯を
水と地表の労わりあいを
峠はすべて懐におさめ
超然として見守っている

北山の道

『平家物語』を朗読する時　私は当時の人間になっている
平清盛は私のふるさとの山を通って　京都の北山の奥へ進んだ
平成の今　私が歩いている山道は　平清盛一行が北へと進んだ同じ
　　山の道
その狭い山道は　平清盛が通っていた道で今の山の道

北山の奥に　清盛の建築工事による古い建造物がある
これは清水寺の舞台の原型
古くからの日本の山岳信仰の強い望みを　私に教えている
平清盛と今　語り合っている　日本の心について

二章

地球温暖化

生態系の異変を
太陽はつぶさに見つめ
地底のマグマは　怒りを日々ためこんでいる
風はため息をつく

人智は　こんなにも残酷な方向へ進むのかと
　　　動植物は嘆き　動転し
地球の神秘のオーラは
核兵器のず太さに接し　年毎に弱くなっていく

「僕たちの国と故郷は　海に沈み
未来には　この大地　無くなるかもしれない」と
大洋の中の悲痛な声　宙をさまよい
文明の進歩と　素朴な命の営みが
〈共生〉の峰をめざす過程で　蟻地獄
志のもとに　かすかな望みと光は　脈うっていて

ノモンハン事件

草原のなす地平線
ゴビ砂漠からの入道雲が　頭上に広がる
立っている大地のかなたに　やはり過去日ソ両国の大衝突が
あった　──ノモンハン事件が──
太平洋戦争の二年前
当時の満州国　モンゴル人民共和国の国境ノモンハン付近での戦争

ノモンハン一帯の国境　日ソ間の係争問題となった昔に　生まれて
いなかったとしても　一九三九年九月に日ソ間で停戦協定が成立し
た日を思い起こさずして　気楽に自然の美しさのみに心をうばわれ
ている事ができようか
大陸への日本の侵略
今の平和がもたらすモンゴルツアーの爽快さのもとで
国境兵士の墓　涙の望郷の声を呈して日々を

シルクロードで待つ花は

幼い時から親しんだ
百日草の紅色が
天山山麓への入口で
待っていた
百日は枯れて朽ちない願いをもつ
一年草の強い葉脈直立させて

子供の頃
次の年への期待の小箱へ
胡麻より細かい黒い種は収まった
紅色　朱色　白っぽい花弁に水晶の露
標高六〇〇メートルの京都の村で
花壇の宴の主人公

湖面高度海抜一九八〇メートルの天池湖を望み
中国ウルムチを経て
野外朗読会をもった夏
当地の百日草は
人々のたぎる熱情を知っていた
慎しく祠を内在し
呼吸は
苦を乗り越える方向へ導いた
ロバの懸命な歩みに合わせ
わが両手も　感謝のリズムを生んでいる

カシュガルでの舞踊　朗読

標高一二〇〇メートルのオアシス都市

着慣れた和服　持つ舞扇
親しんだ曲と　自作詩はステージで歩き出す
京都で記した心音　アジアの大地へと

中国人でガイドのО氏は
大学での専攻　日本文学であった
奥深い胸から朗読される日本の古典
異国で聴く故郷の名作
中国の青年による表現に
日本の古典文学〝ここに健在と〟

中華人民共和国最西端の街で
シルクロードの風に向かい
実現した日中交流の　起伏のステージ
ウイグル人が多い土地の交通の要衝で
国家歴史文化名城に指定されている街の足音
着物の模様に　肉声こもり
「たがいにもとう　文学の深淵へのまなざしを」と

香格里拉で舞う
（シャングリラ）

チベット文化圏の微風が
中国雲南省への旅路に伝えていた
「自治州の州政府から舞を出す
日本からも　一人は代表で歌舞の分野で出て下さい」と

「その準備をして出国ですよ」の言葉に応え
黒の紋付　金色の袴がスーツケースに収まった

アジア詩人会議で　プログラムの一環
舞う京の女は　日中の詩人たちの中
〝何か始まるのか〟との視線受け
色彩豊かな舞台へと
異国であっても　表現するのは日本の武士の志
脈々と伝わる姿を　凛々しく（りり）　深く

舞い終ると　現地の少年が会場の遠くで声を発した
「今の写真　欲しいっ」と切望した
少年は夜を迎えた人々から　早々と姿を消した

送るべき写真は　先方の住所わからず
まだ手許にある
──少年よ　君の日本への関心に　将来花開く日もあるだろう
いや　その実現を夢見ている　私は──

大陸へと天空で動く雲に
少年への　応援歌を託している

舞うステージで

挿し示した扇の先に
人間のたゆみない歩みの行程　希求が広がっていく
生命の喜び　苦悩　思わぬ現実
迎え　一体となり　身は舞い姿に

扇を閉じて身に収める時
共に在った命の炎が
身体をあたためる
血流を新鮮にし　時を刻む

扇はすべてを知っていて
背を押し　心臓を律し
芸術の峰の光を
構築せよ──と

タクラマカン砂漠の少年

西域の旅の途上
熱砂の放つ身をさす光線に
君は　慣れきっているのであろう
大小の鈴を一束にし
鳴らしながら　観光客にどこまでもついて歩き
「千円でーす　買って下さい」と真剣な声

たどたどしい日本語が　離れはしない
絹製品の衣裳を日本で保つ身に
それは〝金属バット〟
夏バテですと故国で言い交わす民衆への
強力な──カンフル注射──

銀色の大小の鈴の束には
古人の渇きがこもっている
砂漠の中をラクダに乗って移動した
大陸の民の想いが満ちている
鳴らせ　小さな手で　タクラマカン砂漠での鈴の音を
真面目なまなざし　笑みをそのままに　子供なりの仕事をこなせ
過去に砂漠を行き来した隊列の苦と　願望を
黙して歩むラクダの吐息を
その鈴は内在している
熱さをものともしない妙なる音色を
君はもつ

三章

オックスフォードへ

パリを経てロンドンに滞在
私は一人オックスフォードまでの電車に揺られていた
向かい合わせのシートの間に
小さな机がある

車内でノートを広げられる
苦労もなく文字も書ける
郊外の線路は国土の香をふくみ
自ずと先人の詩が胸に住む

一七八八年に生まれたショージ・ゴードン・バイロンの声　脊を
　　動かし
あの詩編「シヨンについてのソネット」の冒頭が広がっていく
〝自由よ！　鉄鎖に抗する精神を守る、永遠の霊よ！
お前は牢獄にあってこそ真の生彩を発揮する〟

一八一六年にスイスのシヨン城を訪れたバイロンは記した
シヨン城の牢獄に幽閉されたジュネーブの人・ボンニバードに
政治的自由と宗教の改革を呼んだ魂に
バイロンは　ほとばしる想いを捧げた

人道的な強い心音は　近づく学徒の多い街へ誘い　語る
自由を考えさす道のりで

オックスフォードへの列車内は
動く書斎の　限りある貴重な時間

オックスフォード大で学徒と

校内での静かな午後
長身の学徒は　青い瞳を見開き話す
「世界の国々から来た人と共に学ぶのは　大切だ
おたがいに　国のありのままを話しあいたい
我々はオリエントに関心をもっていても
多くの者は　日本へ行ったことがない
僕らも　できれば東洋の国、日本へ出かけて行くのが望ましい」

「地図の上でも　おたがいに海に囲まれた国——島国
国の歴史について話をすればきりがないが
これから大陸の中の国ではない海に囲まれた国が
どう生きていくか　話しあいたいなぁ
たとえ一個人としての夢であっても」

「今や　海と陸路だけを使って他国へ行く時代ではない
空路を考える時　空の安全を本当に考えるべき時代です
空路の安全　そして慣習　いや国際法を守る事こそ大事ですね
人々の宗教や国の理念が異なっていても　更に理解しあい　人道的
　にも望ましい道を進みたいですね」

京都から来た詩人である一母親と
英国人の若い学徒は
昔からの友人であった如く
話しあい　談笑する五月の空の下

乳房のもとの少年は

コモ湖を訪れた一行に
若さ　老齢　歳の巾広いグループに
瞬間矢のように飛び出して来た
少年

あなたは　最も高齢の日本人男性に擦れ違うふりをして　体当たり
　をして去った
でも　失敗したね
ズボンのポケットの財布は　抜けなかった
執筆する人の長年の時計を付けた鎖と　鍵だけを掬って行って

道端にしっかり座り　乳房を赤ん坊にふくませる母親のもとへ
素早く帰った七〜八歳の年格好
白い肌に褐色の頭髪
小さいジーンズ姿は子供らしくあどけないのに
少年よ　あなたの任務は　その日幾ばくかの現金を掬り取ってくる
　こととは

誰もが悲しい空をもっている
少年よ　母に示せ純な本心を
弟を妹を守れ……まっすぐに
堂々と　天を仰ぐ胸を育て
君は大きくなって信じる仕事を　この世でもって

ジプシーの母子の君に
地にある友愛　確と共に在ることが
〈課題〉

顔と顔を見つめあって
人として
あの山を越えよう

カルチェ・ラタンに日は暮れて

星をたぐり寄せようと　幻の声
カルチェ・ラタンでの夕暮れ時
フランス語　英語　京ことばが合体し
ほっとして座ったパリでの学生街

過去にインタビューをした青年は
〝今　どのような社会人に〟
三十年前　政治学を専攻し
将来「中国　日本を訪れたい」と言っていた

パリ大学の構内でインタビューをした五月
美しい女子学生が隣にいた
彼女と一緒の人生を歩んでいるかもしれない
教授職についているのかも

いや　どのような社会人になっていても
話合ってみたい　日本と日本人についての本音を
今は　確認の手だてがない
フルネーム　大学の卒業年度　はっきりせず

実姉の娘の息子が　昨年パリ大学へ入学した
もし　日本人の私と同じく政治学を専攻していると語りあった日を
記憶の大海から彼が思い出すならば……

不可能か　望むべくもない
人の出会いは星座の星のように
あまりにも輝く不思議さをもっていても
流れゆき

国連本部を訪れて

地雷は　目の前に
丸い形　だいだい色の兵器は展示されていて
対人地雷と聞き　見つめ続ける
話で頭に入っていた地雷は　こういう形か

踏んだ者を爆破　殺傷する物体は
人を殺すというより
大変な負傷をおわせる兵器
戦乱後の地で　土の中に多くひそんでいる今

この恐ろしさを内包して
地球は回っている
撤去の運動が善意の歩みで進んでいても
土中に眠る破壊力は
どのような内なる言葉をもつのか

予測という〈不吉な展開〉
敵の通過が予測される場所に設置
人が踏むと重さで反応
起爆装置についているもの　ワイヤーが引っぱられたり　振動や
　生じる傾斜に反応

ニューヨークの国連本部を訪れ

体に埋まった地雷の姿
全世界に約一億一千万個の地雷が埋まっているという情報に
マンハッタンでの午後は　震えの時間と化していく

ワシントンD.C.で

空路でニューヨークからワシントンD.C.へ行く
現地で待っていた日本人ガイドは　彼の乗用車で訪れる所を話し
　　説明後出発

日本人３人のガイドは　１日中街を案内　国の基本である精神を私
　　は見聞きし歩いた
計画のもとに建てられた人達の街で　パステルカラーの光景と　鴨
　　川のような景色を見ていた
何を見つめ　私は何を思っていたのか

1800 年に建造されたホワイトハウス
ホワイトハウスは白く輝いており　バージニア産のライムストーン
　　で建てられている
初代の大統領であったジョージ・ワシントンは 1972 年にその基礎を
　　築いた

リンカーン記念堂でゲティスバーグアドレスを自然に暗唱していた
「人民の人民による人民のための政治」は英語の勉強を毎日行い始め
　　た日を思い出させる

アーリントン国立基地で国のために働き　すでに故人となっておら
　　れる方々の死を受けとめた
その声は　私の胸に大きくなり　広がる

その声は　共に国を支えた精神の道程を　おごそかに語る

スミソニアン本部の関心があった博物館の宇宙博物館
忘れえない事実　話しきれない思いを抱いた
私は月の石を見　会話をしていた
はてしない大空の　質問をしていた

飛行士が持ち帰った月の石
何故私はそれ程　釘づけにされるのか
人類のもたらす英知
人間が地球で触る事のできなかった物体
想像していた月の表面の石は
どんなに美しく重くても
人間の行為で　月を離れ
私の心に住みついた

パリ大学で

スイスからパリヘ着いた日
やはり訪れたのは　インタビューの約束
パリ大学であった
政治学を専攻している青年が　未来の夢を示した
──一九八七年五月の記述は
今も机の中に──

二〇一五年　父親はフランス人　母親は日本人である若者が
入学したパリ大学で
母のふるさと京都を想う

血がつながっている！
母の母の妹の著書は　以前近くの書店にあった
緑色の表紙で
僕の半分の血は日本　遠くはないよ
ママンの母国　この時代を共に語ろう

あとがき

　2016 年 4 月に、詩集『香格里拉で舞う』を上梓した。その時からアジアの国々や欧米で記してきたかなりの数の詩作品を、英語表現でも残しておきたいと思っていた。

　最近の詩作品と共に『香格里拉で舞う』の中から幾編をも机上に乗せ、日本語で書いていた詩を連日英語表現で記した。一人で机に向う時間内に一日に一編は英語にて書き終える事を課す日が続いた。

　36 年前に第 47 回国際ペン東京大会に出席して以来、世界の文学者達と共に文学の世界大会を持つ状態となり、日英の両語での出版を自ずと志すようになってきた。東アジアでの詩の大会、アジア詩人会議、世界詩人会議で発表をしてきた経験は、やはり今も二年に一回開催の世界詩人会議に参加となり、自作詩の朗読、研究テーマに即した講演、舞台に招かれての日本の舞踏発表を毎回行っている。

　世界情勢は変動し、地球の遠くからの様々な声は、やはり国、社会、人間を考えさせる。

　親しい旧友、いつも共に励んできた詩友、そして世界詩人会議等で共に語り合っている世界の人々のもとへ、当詩集を感謝の気持ちをこめて届けようと思っている。

　この太陽系の惑星の中で、今の時代に共に生きる縁を潔く噛み締め、文化、文明とは何かを胸中にこの地上の森羅万象に更に向き合い、初心にかえっての記述をと望む。

　母校の北垣宗治先生には、英詩発表を志す法学部卒業生の私は、大変お世話になった。そんな北垣先生に最終的に私の詩を翻訳していただいたこと

はとても名誉なことだ。
　またコールサック社の鈴木比佐雄社長、そしてお世話になりましたすべ
ての方々に、心より御礼申し上げる。

　2019 年 11 月 24 日

安森ソノ子

著者略歴

安森ソノ子　やすもりそのこ　（旧姓　藤井ソノ子）

京都市にて出生。
1963 年　同志社大学法学部政治学科卒業。同年より京都大学にて研修。
1960 年〜 2000 年　京都にて研究会「家の会」で研究発表（文学者論等を
　　　　　含む）。後半 2000 年まで世話人代表。
1979 年　詩集『紫蘇を摘む』（ポエトリーセンター）
　　　　　日本図書館協会選定図書となる。
1982 年　『日本現代女流詩人叢書　安森ソノ子詩集』（芸風書院）
1989 年　『安森ソノ子の詩による女声合唱組曲 紫蘇を摘む時』（音楽之友社）
1996 年　詩集『地上の時刻』（編集工房ノア）
1997 年　エッセイ集『京都　歴史の紡ぎ糸』（醂燈社）
2008 年　『安森ソノ子の詩によるソプラノ歌曲集　京都を研ぐ』（舞苑企画）
2016 年　詩集『香格里拉で舞う』（土曜美術社出版販売）
2018 年　電子書籍『香格里拉で舞う』（おいかぜ書房）
　　　　　CD『安森ソノ子の詩による女声合唱曲』『安森ソノ子の詩によ
　　　　　るソプラノ歌曲　京都を研ぐ』発表。

所属
日本ペンクラブ（35 年間会員永年表彰を受ける、元委員）・日本現代詩人会・
日本詩人クラブ・関西詩人協会・現代京都詩話会運営委員・京都市芸術文
化協会・京都日仏協会・NPO 京都コミュニティ放送・英日詩集「パンドラ」
各会員

職歴・活動歴
思想の科学研究会にて執筆、発表、元評議員。
高校と大学の元教員。大学での元図書館長。

パリ大学、オックスフォード大学にて執筆。
現代ジャパン・ゴールド・アカデミー代表。
京都コミュニティ放送の FM79.7 京都三条ラジオカフェにて「安森ソノ子
の詩とエッセイ」を企画、放送中。

詩誌
「呼吸」〝PANDORA〟（日英語にて出版）同人。
元「地球」「柵」終刊。元日本未来派同人。

受賞
2014 年　世界詩人会議にて「優秀詩人賞」「優秀貢献賞」
2018 年　「現代日本文学作家大賞」
2019 年　「フランス芸術文化大賞」

舞踊講師の資格
全日本民俗舞踊連盟公認講師となる（芸名　風月舞苑）、
剣舞の正賀流（雅号　安森文加）、古典舞踊を花柳流にて学ぶ。
能楽の観世流では 20 歳代より舞台に立つ。河村禎二（重要無形文化財保持
者　観世流職分）に師事。現在、河村和重（観世流シテ方　河村能舞台当主）
に師事。

世界詩人会議にて自作詩発表と小講演、日本の舞踊発表を担当。
アジア詩人会議にて、ほぼ毎回参加し、発表する歳月を経る。
住所：〒 603-8124 京都市北区小山下板倉町 29

石炭袋

Yasumori Sonoko Poems in English and Japanese
"TOUCHING MURASAKI SHIKIBU'S SHOULDER"

English translation by Kitagaki Muneharu

First printing February 27, 2020

ISBN978-4-86435-417-2
Published by Coal Sack Publishing Company

Coal Sack Publishing Company
2-63-4-209 Itabashi Itabashi-ku Tokyo 173-0004 Japan
Tel: (03)5944-3258 / Fax: (03)5944-3238 suzuki@coal-sack.com
http://www.coal-sack.com President: Hisao Suzuki

安森ソノ子英日詩集『紫式部の肩に触れ』
Yasumori Sonoko Poems in English and Japanese
"TOUCHING MURASAKI SHIKIBU'S SHOULDER"

2020 年 2 月 27 日初版発行
著　者　安森ソノ子
訳　者　北垣　宗治
発行者　鈴木比佐雄
発行所　株式会社 コールサック社

〒 173-0004　東京都板橋区板橋 2-63-4-209
電話 03-5944-3258　FAX 03-5944-3238
suzuki@coal-sack.com　http://www.coal-sack.com

郵便振替　00180-4-741802
印刷管理　（株）コールサック社　制作部

装丁　奥川はるみ

ISBN978-4-86435-417-2　C1092　￥2000E